This Little Tiger book belongs to:

Harry S

To Thomas James, with love
~ RS
For Mum and Dad
~ GH

LITTLE TIGER PRESS
1 The Coda Centre, 189 Munster Road, London SW6 6AW
www.littletiger.co.uk

First published in Great Britain 2001
This edition published 2016

Text © 2001 Ragnhild Scamell
Illustrations © 2001 Gaby Hansen
Ragnhild Scamell and Gaby Hansen have asserted their rights
to be identified as the author and illustrator of this work
under the Copyright, Designs and Patents Act, 1988.

Printed in China
LTP/1900/1573/0616
1 3 5 7 9 10 8 6 4 2

The Wish Cat

Ragnhild Scamell
Gaby Hansen

LITTLE TIGER PRESS
London

Holly's house had a cat flap.
It was a small door in the
big door so a cat could come
and go.

But Holly didn't have a cat.

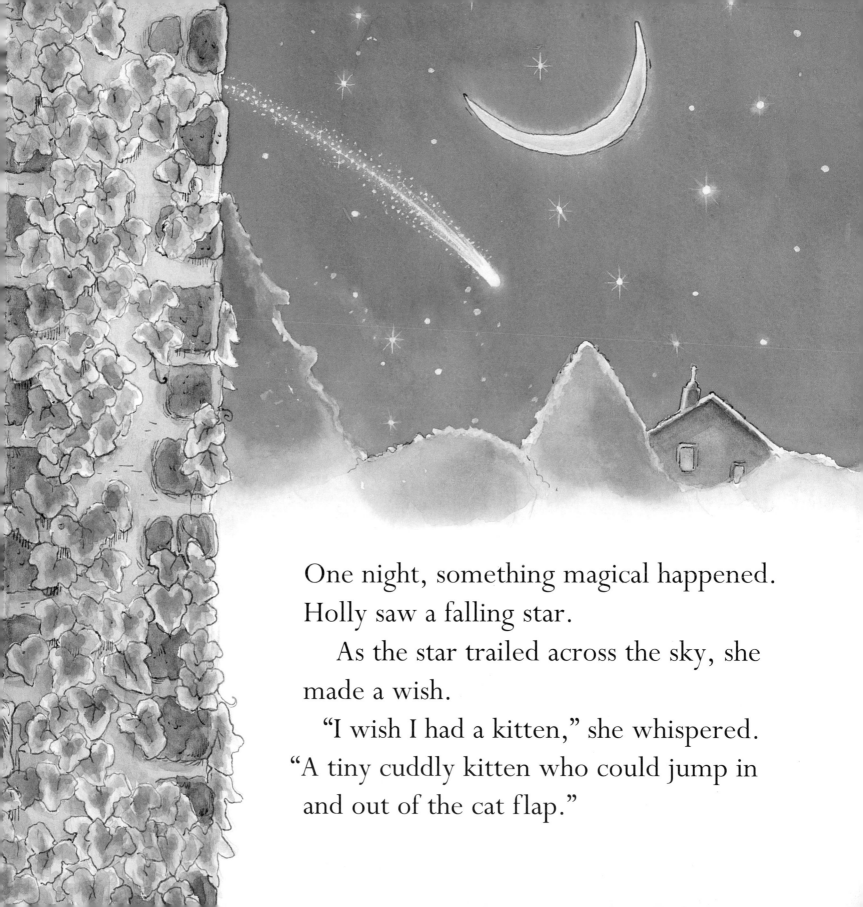

One night, something magical happened.
Holly saw a falling star.

As the star trailed across the sky, she
made a wish.

"I wish I had a kitten," she whispered.
"A tiny cuddly kitten who could jump in
and out of the cat flap."

CRASH!

Something big landed on the window sill outside.

It wasn't a kitten . . .

It was Tom, the scruffiest, most raggedy cat Holly had ever seen. He sat there in the moonlight, smiling a crooked smile.

"Miao-o-ow!"

"I'm Tom, your wish cat," he seemed to say.

"It's a mistake," cried Holly.
"I wished for a kitten."
Tom didn't think Holly had
made a mistake.

He rubbed his torn ear against the window and howled so loudly it made him cough and splutter.

"Miao-o-ow, o-o-w, o-o-w!"

Holly hid under her duvet, hoping that he'd go away.

The next morning, Tom was still
there, waiting for her outside the
cat flap. He wanted to come in,
and he had brought her a
present of a smelly
old piece of fish.

"Yuk!" said Holly. She picked it up and dropped it in the dustbin. Tom looked puzzled. "Bad cat," she said, shooing him away.

"Go on, go home!" said Holly, walking across to her swing.

But Tom was there before
her. He sharpened his
claws on the swing . . .

and washed his coat
noisily, pulling out bits
of fur and spitting them
everywhere.

At lunchtime, Tom sat on the
window sill, watching Holly eat.

She broke off a piece of her sandwich and
passed it out to him through the cat flap.
Tom wolfed it down, purring all the while.

In the afternoon, a cold wind swept through the garden, and Holly had to wear her jacket and scarf. Tom didn't seem to feel the cold. He followed her around . . .

chasing leaves . . .

balancing along the
top of the fence . . .

showing off.

Soon it was time for Holly
to go indoors to tea.
"Bye then, Tom," she said,
and stroked his tatty
head.

Tom followed her across to the door
and settled himself by the cat flap.

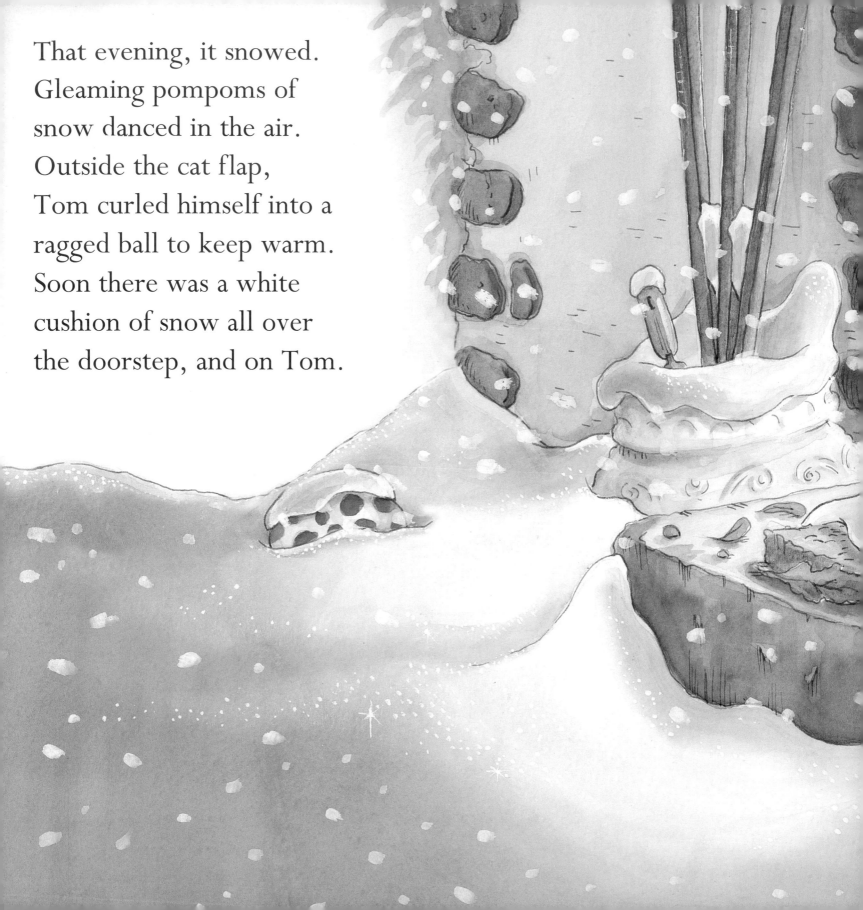

That evening, it snowed.
Gleaming pompoms of
snow danced in the air.
Outside the cat flap,
Tom curled himself into a
ragged ball to keep warm.
Soon there was a white
cushion of snow all over
the doorstep, and on Tom.

Holly heard him miaowing
miserably. She ran to the
cat flap and held it open . . .

Tom came in, shaking snow all over
the kitchen floor.
"Poor old Tom," said Holly.

He ate a large plate of food, and drank
an even larger bowl of warm milk.
Tom purred louder than ever when
Holly dried him with the kitchen towel.

Soon Tom had settled down,
snug on Holly's bed.

Holly stroked his scruffy fur,
and together they watched the
glittering stars.

Then, suddenly, another star
fell. Holly couldn't think of
a single thing to wish for. She
had everything she wanted.
And so had Tom.